THE FOLLOWING DOCUMENTS were found in the home of Petronille Blackstone after her death, by her granddaughter, Mary Augusta Blackstone. They were immediately submitted to the government of New Whiteridge for historical investigation and then acquired by the managers of the Blackstone Estate to be added to their ongoing archive and Museum of New Whiteridge History.

It is noted that Petronille Blackstone specifically stated in her Last Will and Testament that anything related to the Blackstone Manor is officially public property, and she wishes for the home to be open for and owned by the public, not one specific entity. These documents are on loan for your perusal, as a party personally interested in the historical and supernatural properties of Blackstone Manor. It is noted at this time that the government of New Whiteridge takes no stance on whether or not the activities that went on surrounding Blackstone Manor have any sort of supernatural backing to them, and anything stated otherwise is merely conjecture.

It is recommended that the following documents be handled carefully, as many of the archivists for the New Whiteridge museum have reported feeling unwell or lightheaded, specifically after handling any documents related to the Blackstone Estate.

February 14th, 1912
Brunswick, Maine
Transcribed by Viola Descartes, a delightful woman I
met on the train.

My Brother Victor,

It was kind of you to ensure that a letter was
waiting for me upon my arrival into Brunswick. I
appreciate your thoughtfulness, though you made sure to
write it with a pen and paper, making it so that I
needed to ask for help in order to read it. You know
how to write in Braille, or with a pen that will leave
an impression enough on the paper for me to decipher.
There is absolutely no reason to be quite as obnoxious
and rude as you have been. I do not have the energy or
time to find someone to read each of these out to me,
and you know that. Please ensure that all private
letters to me in the future are written in a script
that we can both independently read.

On a more positive note, you need not be as worried
as you detailed. I made it to Maine just fine, and the
train ride was only a little bit bumpy. I know you've
been deeply concerned for my well-being since I left,
and I am delighted to inform you that my state of being
can still be considered "dying" and has not yet
advanced to "actively dead." I only found myself a
little nauseous upon exiting my train car, and my dear
new friend Viola says that she feels it too, so we
decided to attribute it to motion sickness. Though, I
know from experience that it is most likely not motion
sickness. My joints ache as always, and it is days like
this that I am grateful I have my cane to lean on. I
know that sooner rather than later there will come a
day where I will find myself needing a chair to move

around as easily as I do, and though I do not look forward to it, it allows me to better appreciate the days where my cane is all I need.

I shouldn't bother you with all my talk. I know you already worry enough about making sure that our family inheritance is secure once I die. But perhaps that won't be something we have to think about anymore after this journey! If all goes ideally, which it could, there will be a cure waiting for me when I reach my destination. Wherever that is. I believe I am headed to Boston next, at your recommendation. I know you were so opposed to this trip, so it was very kind of you to make a suggestion as to where I might be able to gain more information. And I am very excited to experience more of the world, and even a city! Everything beyond our manor home is so large and inviting, at times I begin to wonder why you were worried at all.

I have my own set of worries though, of course. Do not think I'm not being cautious in all my ventures. Dr. Kinard and I went over the various limitations of my illness several times before I finally got on the train. I know how little time I have left, and I am determined to spend it to the absolute best of my ability. I assure you that if my body begins to weaken, or if I feel the end coming for me, I shall return home as soon as I am capable. I was told that theoretically, if I continue to deteriorate as I have these past months, then I should have anywhere from eight months to a year left of my life. That's plenty of time, I think. And it is a valiant cause, for which I am more than willing to sacrifice some of my strength. This cure isn't really for me, you know. It is for our family. It is for any children you or I may want to have in the future, so that they might not be beset with such frustrations, and can have the future our mother and father wanted for us. The future you or I might want for them.

And I still have so much left to do! I'm certain that by the time I return home, I shall feel delightfully satisfied and ready to pass on whatever there is left to give up. I have my list of accomplishments, and I am checking them off one by one.

I know you were unsettled when I told you about this journey that I decided to take. You said a few choice words to me, none of which were nice. I specifically remember you calling me a disappointment to the entire family. I do hope that you're enjoying your time alone at the house, though. I know your every waking day cannot be consumed by thoughts of where I am going and what I am doing, and so I hope that you can find moments of peace without me there. I know I'm finding my own moments of peace without you every day on my journey.

I will end this letter with a note of optimism. Viola, the one I've noted is transcribing this letter, has informed me that her sister, Lillian, lives in Boston, and has a boarding house there where I can safely stay and be not only accounted for, but cared for. That gives me a little bit of time to settle in and find my way around Boston before I see where I am led next. I do hope I find something there that will benefit me.

I miss you, and I miss home, but I am excited to see more of the world than I ever had before. I can only hope that you're just as excited for me.

Your sister,
Petra

Obituaries

Augusta Ottilie Cates-Blackstone passed away from a long-term illness on Saturday, July 1st, 1911. She was followed in death exactly one week later on July 8th, 1911 by her husband, Simon Victor Blackstone.

The memorial service was held on Monday, July 10th, and was filled with a crowd of friends and loved ones. As lifelong residents of New Whiteridge, their loss is felt deeply by the community. They spent their time doting over their two children, making donations to the city, and shining light into the areas of town that needed it most.

While Simon could often be found in his library reading a book, Augusta spent her spare hours and final days tending to her garden and caring for her daughter.

A service will be held at Blackstone Manor on Wednesday, July 12th. Flowers and other donations should be addressed to Blackstone Manor. The family asks that no monetary donations be made at this time.

They are survived by their two children, Victor Blackstone, 24, and Petronille Blackstone, 20. They are preceded in death by Simon's parents, also former New Whiteridge residents, William and Blanche Blackstone.

February 29th, 1912
Boston, Massachusetts
Transcribed by Mrs. Lillian Rouse, the owner of the
boardinghouse at which I am staying, and Viola's older
sister.

Dear Brother,

   This letter will be a shorter one, as my attention is
occupied by Mrs. Rouse and her delightful tenants. She
has rented me a room on the first floor, for ease of my
joints, and she is making sure that I have three solid
meals a day while I remain in Boston. I am safe here,
and I am making my way to New York City, where I
believe more answers will be found.

   I am greatly excited about the venture to New York,
though. Every moment I've spent in Boston so far has
given me hope for what the world and cities are like.
Everything feels so small, yet I finally feel free. I'm
not even sure if that makes any sense to you, or if
you'll just pass it off as one of my odd, feverish
ravings. At home, silence echoed, and I could feel
every movement any person made through the halls. I
used to count our father's footsteps as he paced in his
office above my bedroom. It was how I went to sleep.

   Boston sings, did you know? I think all cities sing,
maybe, but I can't say much considering this is my
first. Everything is so loud; it's beautiful, and it
drowns out the sound of my cane on the sidewalk. I am
so surrounded by noise that I feel comfortable. I don't
worry about anyone listening to where I'm going or
worrying about my state of being. I am on my own, and
it fills my heart with a sense of confidence I had not
previously realized I was capable of. You called me
foolishly optimistic in your last letter, what with my

hopes of finding a cure for our family, but the city air seems to be clearing my lungs more than I had realized it could.

I know you're afraid for me, as is your right to be. You are my guardian now, and I understand how stressful that must be considering it isn't something you had ever been prepared for. I know Mother and Father didn't exactly die suddenly, but it isn't as if we could have been ready for it when it happened. No one could have been prepared for that sort of thing.

But truly, I am feeling better.

You also mentioned in your previous letter your desire to marry me off to a nice man to ensure that the inheritance has somewhere to go once I die. I know you're a little bit wounded that the money (is it money? I never saw the will) was not left for you to spend as you like, but I assure you, in my hands it will be safe and secure, and you will never be without. There's no need to marry me off to one of your college pals simply because you know that he would share with you what you assume I wouldn't. Do you really think me so selfish? I have our best interests at heart. Trust me, as you are asking that I trust you.

Besides, I have no desire to even get married anytime soon. I had always assumed I never would. Either my illness would take me, or I would simply be your Madeline Usher. What a horrid fate for the both of us, isn't it? Myself, buried alive in a coffin, and you, tormented by nothing more than my existence.

This is getting morbid, so I will release Mrs. Rouse from her bond in writing this and go about my day. I assure you, you shall hear from me again soon.

Yours,
Petra.

A selection from the

Last Will & Testament of Simon & Augusta Blackstone

SECOND: We give all tangible personal property owned by us at the time of our death, including, without limitation, personal effects, clothing, jewelry, furniture, furnishings, household goods, and vehicles, together with all insurance policies relating thereto, to our child Petronille Ottilie-Cates Blackstone, who survives us.

THIRD: We give all the rest, residue and remainder of our property and estate, both real and personal, of whatever kind and wherever located, that we own or to which we shall be in any manner entitled at the time of my death (collectively referred to as our "residuary estate"), to our child Victor Simon Blackstone, who survives us.

FOURTH: Under the circumstance that our child, Petronille Ottilie-Cates Blackstone, is either deceased or taken care of (definition specified below) at the time of reading this will, anything given to her is to be thenceforward given to our child, Victor Simon Blackstone.

FIFTH: The definition of "taken care of" in reference to this Will and in reference to our daughter, Petronille Ottilie-Cates Blackstone, is as follows: she must be without want, she must be married to someone who will care for her in any condition, she must be in no financial duress at any point in time. Additionally, should these conditions not be met or become impossible to meet due to Petronille's failing health, Victor should ensure that her current life and the remainder of her days are comfortable and without any stress or circumstance that could worsen her condition.

SIXTH: Regarding the inheritance that comes with the property, over which we have no control. This is to be granted to whomever the property decides, and whomever is presiding over the property at any given point in time. We acknowledge again that we have no control over this, and the house decides to whom that particular inheritance is granted.

March 8th, 1912
New York, New York
Transcribed by Leona Cahill, a delightful secretary
with the New York Public Library.

Dear Victor,

   Honestly, brother, you need to calm down. Perhaps it
isn't my place to say, but your anger is unfounded and
pointless. I will not be returning home any time soon
and that is that. If you continue to berate me in such
ways as you are, I assure you that never again will my
presence grace the halls of Blackstone Manor. And you
can count on that.

   I apologize for the potentially overdramatic nature
of that statement, but it is true. We're all going to
die someday, but your insistence that my death is
literally around the corner is unfounded and
frustrating. Mere weeks ago I had assumed the same as
you -that perhaps this effort was futile and my travels
would only make me weaker. I do not believe this
anymore, as my resolve has only strengthened the
further I go and the longer I spend away from home.

   Regardless, I am learning, I am growing, as is my
way. Ms. Cahill has assisted me in finding some old
business records having to do with our grandparents'
paper mill. There wasn't much to be had, but she has a
cousin of some sort in Philadelphia who is greatly
invested in this sort of thing. She's going to give me
his information and reach out to him via telegraph to
let him know that I would like to meet with him to
discuss. I am feeling hopeful today, and that delights
me.

   I recognize that your anger is most likely rooted in
worry for my well-being. But trust me, Victor, all will

be well in time. I am capable of taking care of myself, and this world is not so dangerous as you made it seem. One might think that you didn't want me to find a cure, with the way you're going on about everything.

But I know you want what's best for me, right? After all, you are so stalwart about ensuring that I believe that you have my health at the forefront of your mind, and that's the only reason you're suggesting all of this. It couldn't be anything else, could it?

I will admit to you that I do get homesick, on occasion. The library here, the way it smells, reminds me of our own in Blackstone Manor. I wish that I had the capability to read the books, but perhaps it wouldn't be so bad to have someone read them to me. I don't remember the last time I actually sat down and read a book. Perhaps it was Alice's Adventures in Wonderland. I couldn't have been more than six or seven, so most likely it was Mother who read it to me. I wasn't quite as sick then as I am now, as you know, but even then my sight was dreadful.

How appropriate, though. I'm not even certain that's what it was, but this is what I'm choosing to believe. I've always been a bit of an Alice, haven't I? Wandering around in our forests and digging up all sorts of holes in the ground, no matter how much mother and father scolded me. I hold this comparison close, brother. It helps me feel better about leaving.

Not that I'm having second thoughts, because I'm not. I'm still more than happy to have left home, and I am so pleased with all the people I've been meeting and learning from. It's only that sometimes, I catch the scent of a pine tree on the air and it makes me wish I were in the forests surrounding the house. It is still cold, but I would greatly enjoy the crunch of snow under my feet in this moment.

I'm sorry to hear that you aren't feeling well, brother. The headaches and the night terrors really are nothing to balk at, and I suggest you be careful and take care of yourself. Your implication that it could be related to stress on the mind seems plausible to me, and the only solution to stress is rest. You aren't quite as used to spending so much time in that house as I am, and it can be a heavy thing on the mind. I wish that there were more I could do from here, but my main suggestion should it worsen would be to call my personal doctor. You've always been insistent that you can power through any trial or tribulation, so I'm sure you won't call any doctor until things become unbearable. But that's fine, and hopefully it won't last long enough to get worse. Our family is so used to misfortune when it comes to illness, so it is unusual for us to deal with an average cold. I'm certain your headache won't progress at the rate that my own illness has, if that's your concern. Things seem to get worse for me, but you're typically exempt from that, aren't you?

I beg you, please don't be angry with me, though. I am doing my best, and I only hope that you're as proud of me as I am of myself. I know you're a bit averse to change, and I respect that, but you also need to respect that I am an entirely different person from you. It hurts me that you believe that I am incapable of taking care of myself, and also that you wish to keep me confined. Whether I find any solutions or not, I am still your sister, and you are still my brother. (Though, to be perfectly honest, the lead from Ms. Cahill's cousin makes me think that the end is in sight. Not my end, and maybe not in sight for me, but you understand what I mean).

Say hello to the trees for me,
Petra

The Baltimore Daily　　　　　*August 13, 1859*

Spiritualism Sweeps Baltimore!

The dead speak! The city of Baltimore was recently visited by three very special young ladies, Kate, Maggie, and Leah Fox. These three women possess an unparalleled ability that is grabbing the attention of everyone in town —the ability to converse with the dead! Our reporters found themselves at one of the Fox Sisters' opulent displays of talent, and reported it as follows:

The evening at the Fox Sisters' show began as a relatively normal conversation— the three girls sat around a table, discussing with the audience and with each other their relationship to the dead. After a while, there began a soft knocking from the underside of the table. The eldest sister, Maggie, explained this to be a spirit that had come to converse with someone in the crowd. She asked if anyone present had lost a family member within the past twelve months, and a young woman stood, declaring that her mother had passed about three months ago, and she was certain that the spirit was for her. The young woman was later identified as Blanche Blackstone, a Baltimore native.

The sisters proceeded to ask Blanche questions about the life of her mother, providing leading details and making gentle suggestions about what Blanche ought to say. After a period of time, the lights in the theatre flickered out. This was met with much loud discussion from the audience. Over the din, a voice, wavering and old, called out to Mrs. Blackstone, speaking in what sounded like some form of Latin or Greek. No translation was provided.

The lights came back on, and Mrs. Blackstone was found unconscious on the floor, propped up by her husband, who had attended the whole affair with her. They were quickly escorted out of the theatre, where reporters from the Daily Clipper did their best to retrieve some sort of comment. While Mrs. Blackstone was in no state to be speaking to anyone, her husband did have a few choice words to say regarding the validity of the three women, which the Clipper would prefer not to put in print.

It has yet to be proven whether or not the Fox Sisters are true spiritual mediums, or whether the Blackstone couple were actors hired by them to prove a point, but this reporter remains to be convinced. The Baltimore Daily Clipper remains firmly on the side of the Lord, and should the dead choose to return and speak with the voices of the living, it will be a dark day indeed.

April 13th, 1912
Philadelphia, Pennsylvania
Transcribed by Dr. Edmund Montague, who continues to be an immense help to me.

Victor,
    You will not believe how delightful I'm feeling today. I think the travel has done me good. My bones feel stronger than they have in months, and while I don't think my cough will ever entirely go away, I am able to take full breaths with relative ease! I know you fear that my taking this trip unescorted was a danger to not only my health but also my safety, and I'm sure that upon the return of your friend that visited me, a brief examination of his person will prove to you that I am more than capable of caring for

myself. It was nice of you to send someone to collect
me, though. Your thoughtfulness knows no bounds.
(Please note my insincerity.)

I recognized him as one of yours because he refused
to take off that stupid Exeter class ring. I could feel
it when he attempted to grab me. It's that ridiculous
lion's head that always gives it away. You'd think that
your boys would move beyond secondary school,
considering most of them have been through college now,
but I suppose they can't help where they peaked, can
they? Unfortunately he will need to see a doctor, as
his arrival at my hotel rooms did frighten me, and I
might've fractured a bone or two in his face, what with
all my flailing. It's no bother, though, nothing
permanent. He'll be pretty again in a few weeks, I
should think. I would also like to mention that it was
incredibly rude of him to assume he could sneak up on
me just because I cannot see. There is absolutely
nothing wrong with my hearing, and his shoes were
disgustingly loud against the wooden floors of my hotel
room.

Often I delight in how much people underestimate me.
Your folly is not just in assuming that I'm incapable
because I am weak and blind, but also I am your sister,
a young woman, so surely I could be no better than you
in any way, correct? It would do you well not to assume
things like that again. It would do your friends well,
at least. They would more often be left without broken
cheekbones and noses.

I'm beginning to assume that you know more than
you're letting on. Well. Perhaps I shouldn't lie. I do
firmly believe you're keeping information from me,
considering how deeply you underestimate my ability. I
know I cannot see, but that does not mean I am

undeserving of the truth. And it also does not mean that I am anywhere near a fool. In fact, by now, I consider myself to be far less foolish than even you. Maybe once I considered myself weak as well, but I was full of self-doubt. Leaving home was perhaps one of the most terrifying things I've ever done, but now I cannot fathom never having done it. I'm certain you don't recognize the importance of my actions, having taken leave and journeyed away constantly throughout our childhood, but I am content to appreciate my own accomplishments.

Changing the subject to something far more interesting, though; I met up with Ms. Cahill's cousin-or-other, the historian from Philadelphia. He believes he has some documents that connect to our family name. You wouldn't happen to know anything about this, would you? I suppose not, or at least I surely hope not, as then you would have been deliberately keeping something from me. Regardless, considering he is transcribing this letter for me now, I can assume that he intends to maintain my friendship. He has been immensely useful to me in matters relating to mine and Mother's illness, as well as the history of our family line in general. Well, I suppose I cannot call it Mother's illness anymore, can I? Dead people cannot take ill.

Though, like I said, above, I am beginning to feel quite a deal better than I have in the past. Dr. Montague and I went for a walk earlier, and, while I did still need my cane, I hardly felt dizzy, and the coughing was minimal. Edmund was there to offer me his arm if I felt weak, and I did feel inclined to take it on occasion. Philadelphia is such a beautiful place, though I'm told I'll enjoy Baltimore just as well (if not more so than here). Perhaps I'll even feel so moved as to rent a little apartment of my own and live there for a while. What a nice thing it is, to actually feel as though you have a future!

I'm deeply sorry to hear that your condition is not improving. You say you are experiencing headaches, of a more intense degree than you're sure I've ever felt? I'm certain I cannot imagine what that must be like for you. Personally, I recommend sitting in the dark with a nice, cool rag over your face.

The dreams, though, I cannot explain. Should we be in reversed positions, I might suggest the diagnosis of some form of hysteria. I mean, really, hearing voices echoing through the halls? Swearing that our deceased mother and father are watching you sleep? You sound paranoid! As I mentioned before, and as you seem desperate to believe, it is most likely related to stress. Keep to this belief, and get some rest.

I would also like to mention that it is entirely unfounded of you to suggest that your condition is due to my refusal to come home. The stress theorized cannot entirely be because of me, and I've made my position clear. I believe that I am on the edge of discovering something important about myself and about our family, therefore, I shall not be returning to you until I have some semblance of answers.

The records are leading us to Baltimore, which is honestly where I should have gone first, considering that's where our grandparents moved from. Though, now that I'm thinking on it, it was at your suggestion that if I was going to travel, I should go to Boston. Were you intentionally trying to mislead me? I am confused now, and should you actually read this letter instead of carelessly responding with something angry, I wish to know the answer. Did you think that telling me to go to Boston, where you knew I would find no answers, would truly break my spirit and get me to come home? Now that I'm remembering, you seemed surprised when you learned of my intentions to go to New York. What were your words exactly? Ah, yes: "It is unnecessary and dangerous that you travel more. I am certain that you will find nothing, and it is in everyone's best interest that you return home immediately."

How could you be so certain? Unless you were certain that instead of finding nothing, New York would lead me to where I am now. Which is exactly what it did. What are you so afraid of me finding? Why do you hate the possibility of a cure so much as to purposefully give me false information to get me to come home? Do you not also dream of prosperity for our lineage? I would have thought that would be your first concern-not having children that ended up the same as your pitiful sister. I know that if you actually read this letter, you'll accuse me of paranoia, and use that as another excuse for me to return to you. At this point I am not so foolish to believe that your concern is legitimate. It is a bold claim to make, but I'm starting to believe you worry more about the fact that if I die, the possibility exists that I leave my inheritance to someone other than you.

The inheritance, mind you, that I still don't know anything about. What does it entail? I know our family is wealthy, but it can't be much more than the house, can it? I might as well be talking to a brick wall, I know. You told me that I wouldn't see a penny of that money until I was married. You're lucky I haven't spoken to our parents' lawyers about that, because I'm sure they'd have a word or two to say.

I don't actually care about all of that, though. What I care about is that I feel like I am finally steady on my feet. What I care about is that, despite the fact that you told me I never could, I am making friends, and a life for myself away from that house and those walls. I care that I am my own, individual woman, and I am learning that I'm more than you ever thought I could be.

This is where it ends, for now,

Petra

The Telegraph-Journal   January 23rd, 1862

Paper Mill Purchased! A New Dawn For New Whiteridge Property

If you've been recently bothered by the sound of construction on the property across from the paper mill, fear not! The New Whiteridge Paper Processing Plant has been purchased by a young upstart from Baltimore by the name of William Blackstone! He states that he and his wife are delighted to be moving to New Whiteridge to begin the next stage of their lives, and if he can bring some sense of industry and innovation to our town, he will be all the prouder for it.

The property had been recently declared derelict, but Mr. Blackstone has high hopes for what this means for his own future, and for the future of innovation here in New Whiteridge. If you've been following the story of the Paper Mill Property, which we in the Telegraph-Journal have reported on more than once, then you'd be aware that the property has been on the market for years, and had been previously assumed to be cursed by superstitious locals. "The fact of the matter," says Mr. Blackstone, "is that no one here has enough classic American elbow grease to get things done. Sometimes certain properties take a little more work than others, but I'm ready and willing to build my house and provide jobs for this delightful place."

We here in New Whiteridge welcome the Blackstone family, and hope that this marks the sign that good things are headed our way.

A Correspondence from the Former Groundskeeper of the Blackstone Estate to William Blackstone, Shortly After the Land was Purchased

Mr. William,

I appreciate your enthusiasm regarding the paper mill property, and your willingness to go ahead with the business and with working the land. There are a few things of note that we need to discuss before you consider taking on more employees, and, as I've noticed you have a little boy running around, I would feel guilty not bringing it up.

The family that owned the land before you, the Fletchers, have all passed away, as I'm sure you're aware. There seemed to have been some familial predisposition that afflicted them, which causes some people in the town to feel a certain way about the property. They fear that the Fletchers might've cursed the land, or left something terrible behind when they all died. I'm not partial to this belief, but I do have a few warnings for you before you all move in.

You'll notice that there are some specific places where the trees appear to be a little bit weaker, and refuse to grow the same as the ones around them. Don't let your little ones near those areas, if you can help it. From what I understand, there's something in the dirt that might be poisoning them, and might've contributed to the hurt of the Fletchers. I'll do my best to continue investigating and bringing the trees back to life to keep the property as beautiful as I can, but *please note that the effort might be futile, because some things just refuse to grow here, not for lack of trying.*

We've also gotten some reports of some of the maids hearing voices throughout the home itself, or suffering from night terrors while staying the evening. Now, I don't know if you're used to living in a big house like this one, but there can be all sorts of mysterious noises and bumps in the night. Nothing to be worried about. If you hear anything, please let me know, and I'll be happy to investigate the attic for rats, or any other creature that might've tried to make a home up there. It's not uncommon, and definitely contributes to the sounds the maids have been reporting, which are probably what cause their minds to wander to the point of night terrors.

If you're the God-fearing type like the rest of us, there are a few in New Whiteridge who have offered to say a prayer on the land for you, and for your family's health. Please let me know if this is something that would be of interest. My wife and I are members of the local Presbyterian Association, and we would be more than happy to arrange it.

Yours truly,
Franklin Albert Taylor
Groundskeeper

April 27th, 1912
Baltimore, Maryland
Transcribed by Dr. Edmund Montague again, whom I now consider a friend.

My Dearest Brother, Victor Blackstone,
    If you're worried about facing the same end as was once certain of your little sister, I assure you that your eyes will not go first. I had weak eyes from birth, they were susceptible to infection and were sure to

fail me regardless of whether or not I had ever been diagnosed with the illness that plagues us through adulthood (however, now more you than me, it seems). You would know this if you had ever paid attention to me as a child. Alas, here we are, and I shall now describe to you in detail how you will face your end.

Knowing you, first you will lose your ability to concentrate. Your nerves were always far, far weaker than my own, and this will prove a disadvantage here, because what little mental power you had in the past will surely leave you as you deteriorate. You will become weak and nauseous, and I think perhaps you will find yourself vomiting a lot more than you have in the past. You might also find that you can no longer work in the sunlight, as it hurts your eyes and causes the nausea to worsen. It will be hard for you to get up some days, because even taking several steps will feel as though your head has spun right off of your spine.

And speaking of your spine, what a lovely segue. I like to think that perhaps one day you will wake up, and it will be an effort to get out of bed. Every movement will hurt, and you will think back on the days that you called me frail because my pain was to the point where I needed a wheelchair to get around. I know I'm not frail, just as you will know you aren't frail when it happens. But Brother, will your friends remain as jovial and accepting as they are of you currently when you can no longer go hunting? When you can no longer hold a pen for more than minutes at a time, and need someone to manage your correspondence? Will you have any regrets when you visit the graves of our mother and father and think about their final moments, how much pain they must have been in when they passed, and how that is sure to be your future?

Your head will ache, but we discussed this. Eventually your eyes will go, as mine did, and your world will shift to a constant shade of deep, dark gray. Your skin will be like fire to the touch, and you will not want to eat. All food will feel like ash in your mouth.

I speak from experience. Do you regret treating me poorly? Do you regret selling me off, now that you know what's coming?

Ah. I have exposed my knowledge. I'm sure you were wondering what shifted, as now my letters have taken on a more accosting tone. I was never a nice little sister, but it was out of character in the past for me to list off how I believe your body will crumble. Your friend, you know, the "delightful man whom you've asked to become my husband" reached out to me, and I received his correspondence late last week. The poor thing, he felt terrible and told me your entire plot. I can't say I was terribly surprised. It's good to know that some of your friends are better people than expected, though. Henry did tell me he would take decent care of me and be a wonderful husband despite the circumstances, though, should I still wish to marry him after knowing it was all your doing. Not that I'm in particular need of someone to care for me. My bones have grown strong as yours weaken, and my resolve is as impenetrable as it ever was. I consider the hard-headedness our father impressed upon me as a child to be quite the gift these days.

Can I ask, Brother, if I hadn't died at the end of your expected timeline for me, would you have had him poison me? Had him watch as I succumbed to the worst of what the Blackstone Estate had to offer, signing over some dreadful form of legal control over my person that

I had no true say in? I know from experience that you aren't the waiting type, so I'm sure that sitting around impatiently hoping for me to die in my bed is not something you would have wanted to do.

I suppose you must be wondering how I've figured it all out. How I now know that the longer I spend away from home, the more well I become, and the more ill you fall. How I know that when you were away at Exeter, or hunting, or whatever other dreadful things you did with your friends, you were well and you were strong, and I suffered because I could not leave. And now that I am away learning, and traveling, and all other manner of things, you are at home, and your illness worsens.

It's the proximity, Victor. It always has been.

But I'm getting ahead of myself. Perhaps you remember a Dr. Montague from my last letter, the historian? He sent me to Baltimore to some historical records in the public library, and they had quite a lovely amount of information regarding our family there, wouldn't you know it. It was all far too complicated for me to fully understand, and, frankly, if I can't understand it, I know you won't be able to, so I'll do you the liberty of keeping it brief. I'll begin by asking a question: did you ever stop to wonder why our family left Baltimore? It's truly hard to say for certain, but it could be one of two things.

First, one could attribute it to the rise of Spiritualism. As you may or may not know, our grandparents were heavily involved with spearheading the movement in Baltimore as a whole. But of course, people were afraid of it. The majority of people in Baltimore are naturally God-fearing, and it didn't take very long for the rumors to begin to spread about some sort of curse that had wormed its way into our grandparents' hearts. Ghosts tend to stick to people, I'm sure you've heard, and apparently one of the ones that had been called on was… particularly angry. It wanted to watch our family suffer, for whatever reason, and it was inclined to cling to us no matter where we went. And when our grandparents ventured so far as Canada to escape, the spirit decided that it would kill us off, very, very slowly. Allow us to get just a glimpse of life, just enough to fall in love, before ripping away our faculties and eventually the spark itself.

Or, if you find yourself being in that God-fearing category and do not want to believe in things that go bump in the night, you can examine the second option.

Baltimore was an expensive place to live, and our family was running out of money. Perhaps you don't want to admit to yourself that the Blackstone name could have ever wanted for anything, but it's true. And so, Grandmama and Grandfather moved away to Canada, to start work because they purchased a paper mill. And along with the mill, they eventually built the manor. (I know that you're aware of all of this, but trust me, it's pertinent that I go over it again for dramatic effect.) The property our grandparents built the manor on was far cheaper than it should be, and do you know why? People said the land was sick. Poisoned by something beyond our current human understanding. I'm still not sure what they meant by that, but apparently, all who had tried to build or raise families on it had eventually fallen violently, tragically ill. Does that sound familiar to you? There's a science behind it, I'm sure. There's a science behind everything. I don't trust you to give a damn about the science, but it's on my list of things to figure out.

Whichever story you prefer to believe, it all ends up the same. But, based on what you've told me in your letters, and what I'm feeling now, I'm personally more inclined to believe the second. It seems to make sense that if the land itself is corrupted in some way, then eventually those living on it would fall weak to that same corruption. The more time I spend away from the land, the better I become. The more time you spend on it, as the sole victim… the inheritor, as it were, of that corruption, well. The more ill you become. And you can't leave. It would mean leaving behind your life, your friends, and any semblance of the life and fortune you might've started building for yourself. The catch of the entire fortune is that you have to stay there. And so you will.

Unlike you, I have a choice. You will look up at the sky tonight and see the tops of the trees that surround our manor home. The trees I watched you climb as a child, when I could still watch things, in the forest that had always inspired freedom for me. But the trunks to you will feel like prison bars. You will see the sky and feel its weight upon your shoulders. I will look at the same sky, holding the same stars, and even though I will not be able to see it, I know it will be calling to me, which is what I find the saddest. Not your impending loss of life. Not the fact that you wanted to sell me off to a friend because you knew I would die and you could collect our parents' fortune for yourself. Simply the fact that I will never again be able to write on my own, or look into the eyes of a dear friend, or see the trees and the vastness of the world around me.

But I suppose that doesn't even matter, really, because I've been just fine on my own, much to your disbelief. I renounce it all, and I know that I am strong. I will not only exist, but thrive, in this world that has done its best to rid itself of me. I will not be left to the same fate as Mother and Father. That fate is reserved for you, and you alone. Enjoy it while you can. It will not last.

Your sister until the end,
Petronille Ottilie-Cates Blackstone

Obituaries

Victor Simon Blackstone was a driven and hardworking man known throughout the community for his ambition and care for his family. He left this world suddenly on May 26th, 1912, at the age of 24. He was a loving brother, son, and member of the community.

Victor was born to Simon and Augusta Blackstone on January 9th, 1888. After graduating from Phillips Exeter Academy, he returned to New Whiteridge to take over the Blackstone family paper mill and business. His physical health was never in question, and his death took the community by tragic surprise.

He is survived by only his sister, Petronille Blackstone.

There will be no service. He is to be buried without recognition in an unknown location. Do not send flowers to the Blackstone residence, as there will be no one there to receive them.

Author's Note

Dear Reader,

This was one of the first pieces of short fiction I attempted when I started seriously considering writing as a career, and I'm endlessly grateful to Archive of the Odd for allowing it to find a home in such phenomenal company. It came to me when I left behind the world of theatre for the comfort of the page, so it is only appropriate that the story itself ends with what I consider to be Petra's true beginning, as it was just as much my own beginning as well.

It is my hope that people will connect with Petra as much as I did while writing her, through her quiet strength, persistence, and desire to be more than what her remaining family assumes of her.

You are more than the circumstances that define your childhood. You deserve to take up space, and become the sort of monster that you wish to see in the world. Don't let Victor tell you otherwise.

About the Author

Dori Lumpkin is a queer writer and storytelling enthusiast from South Alabama. Their work has appeared in The Deeps, Crow & Cross Keys, and Demons & Death Drops, (amongst others). They love all things speculative and weird, and strive to make fiction writing a more inclusive place. You can find them @whimsyqueen on most social media websites, or check out their website: https://dorilumpkin.carrd.co

Content Warnings

Ableism, chronic illness

About the Publisher

Archive of the Odd is a micropress specializing in speculative found-fiction, run by Cormack Baldwin. It publishes short fiction in the magazine Archive of the Odd.

* 9 7 9 8 9 8 8 4 8 2 7 1 0 *